What grown-ups are saying about ClubZone Kids

"In today's world, where our children are inundated by negative and amoral mess___ ___, the ClubZone Kids books infuse positive, Christian thought___ ___ ___ ___ ___ration. I h___ ___ recommend these books with enth___

> ___ Pediatric neurosurgeon Benjamin S.
> ___on, best-selling author of *Gifted Hands*
> ___ focus of a Today's Heroes series book

> ___ brings godly principals to life for
> ___ into warm human stories that

> ___l Myers, best-selling author of *The*
> ___ *___edible Worlds of Wally McDoogle*
> and *McGee and Me*

> ___ad tells how things just some-
> ___ries is given in a manner that
> ___vhile unfolding in a clear way
> ___cellent job of dealing with
> ___os of children."
>
> —Ken Smitherman, president,
> Association of Christian
> Schools International

Books in the ClubZone Kids series:

Critter Sitters

& Other Stories
That Teach Christian Values

Joel Thompson

Baker Books

A Division of Baker Book House Co
Grand Rapids, Michigan 49516

© 2002 by Joel Thompson

Published by Baker Books
a division of Baker Book House Company
P.O. Box 6287, Grand Rapids, MI 49516-6287

Printed in the United States of America

Library of Congress Cataloging-in-Publication Data

Thompson, Joel, 1952–
    Critter sitters & other stories that teach Christian values / Joel Thompson.
        p. cm. —(ClubZone kids ; 3)
    Summary: Eight stories featuring the ClubZone Kids teach about God
and biblical values, as well as how to apply those teachings to everyday life
at home, church, and school.
    ISBN 0-8010-4511-8 (pbk.)
    1. Christian children—Religious life—Juvenile literature. 2. Christian
life—Juvenile literature. [1. Christian life.] I. Title. II. Title: Critter sitters
and other stories that teach Christian values. III. Series: Thompson, Joel,
1952– . ClubZone kids ; 3.
BV4571. 3.T47 2003
248.8'2—dc21   2002009506

For current information about all releases from Baker Book House, visit our
web site:
                    http://www.bakerbooks.com

Interior design by Brian Brunsting

To
Jaylen, Jeziah, Romeo, Kyle,
and
Deja, Symphony, Nichole
From Poppie

CLUBZONE KIDS
Cast of Characters

Carlos has one big dream . . . to just "fit in!" But, as Carlos will be the first to admit, he has a lot of growing up to do.

Danny calls himself the King of Fun! He is a born leader! Well . . . when he wants to be.

Heather is not shy! Everyone knows she loves to be the center of attention. A real social butterfly, but one with a kind heart.

Natasha is an artistic, active little girl who sometimes doesn't think things all the way through. But, hey, she's working on it!

Michael is one of the most level-headed kids in the neighborhood. Everyone thinks he'll be President of the United States one day.

. . . & others . . .
Phillip, Melissa, Sheela, Timmy, Kevin

Contents

Dear Parents

After working for more than sixteen years to impart faith in God and biblical values to young people, I've learned that Christian character begins at a parent's knee.

The ClubZone Kids series was created for this—so the virtues of Christlike character can be imparted by loving parents in fun, personal, entertaining, and lasting ways at home, church, and even school.

Each book in the series features eight short stories that follow the ClubZone Kids through adventures in their everyday lives. Especially designed for six- to eight-year-olds, books in the series can be read by you to young listeners or by the children themselves. Watch and see how your kids identify with characters in the series and actually begin to live the good values being taught!

In this volume, children will see how to

- use their gifts
- follow Jesus
- give
- love one another
- persist
- be a witness
- recognize and yearn for heavenly rewards, and
- especially love an enemy

So while you'll find books in the series a valuable tool for conveying important life principles in delightful, interesting ways, your children will find the stories memorable and just plain fun. The idea's simple, really, but the goal life-giving: Encourage children to develop their understanding of God's big truths and to incorporate his virtues and values into their own lives!

Your friend,

Joel Thompson

Dear Readers

Do you know what's really awesome about life? Every day you get to make new choices! YOU get to decide how each chapter in the story of your life will turn out! Sometimes, you hit the ball right out of the park and—home run! Other times, you might fumble or, to be honest, blow it . . .

Welcome to the ClubZone!

In the ClubZone, you will meet Danny, Michael, Heather, Natasha, and Carlos, who probably do the same sorts of things you do. But you won't just meet them—you will get to live with them, go to school with them, and try their adventures too. That's when you'll see that you're not the only one with ups and downs!

So come on and join the fun. You're only a page away from entering the ClubZone!

Your friend,

Joel Thompson

Critter Sitters

A Story about Using Your Gifts

Mr. Cobble loved animals. He loved them so much that when he was a young man, he bought a pet store. Every day, he took care of the fish, the parakeets, the hamsters, the kittens, the puppies. And all of the kids in the neighborhood loved to go to Mr. Cobble's pet store and look at the animals.

But now, even though Mr. Cobble still loved animals very much, he was getting too old to take care of them. He decided to sell his pet store and move to someplace warm.

So little by little, Mr. Cobble sold his pets. Pretty

soon, the only animals left were five goldfish, two rabbits, and one leaping lizard.

"My goodness," he said to himself, "what should I do with these pets that I have left?" He thought for a moment. "I know!" he said excitedly. "I'll give them away to some of the boys and girls in the neighborhood!"

So Mr. Cobble found three kids to take the animals: Carlos, Heather, and Natasha.

Carlos liked the goldfish. He watched them swim around in their bowl and made fish-faces at them.

"Would you like to take the five goldfish?" Mr. Cobble asked Carlos.

"Sure!" Carlos said. "I'll take good care of them."

"I know you will," Mr. Cobble said with a twinkle in his eye.

Heather liked the rabbits. She watched them wiggle their noses and tried to wiggle her nose too.

"Heather, what about you?" Mr. Cobble asked. "Will you take the two rabbits?"

"Sure!" Heather said. "I love rabbits. They're so furry and cute."

"You know, Heather," Mr. Cobble said, "I agree with you."

Natasha liked the leaping lizard. She watched him stick out his long tongue and stuck out her tongue too.

"And Natasha, what about the leaping lizard?" Mr. Cobble asked.

"Sure!" Natasha said. "You can count on me."

Mr. Cobble was very happy to find homes for the pets. "Now, take good care of them," he said. "These pets are counting on you for their survival. Hopefully one day I'll be able to come back and see how the pets are doing."

Carlos took his five goldfish home. He found a nice aquarium, filled it with water, and put the fish in it. He loved to feed them fish flakes and watch them swim to the top of the water to eat. Carlos took such good care of the fish that they multiplied. Soon he had an aquarium full of goldfish.

Heather took her two rabbits home. Her dad put together a cage, and she placed the rabbits in it. Heather loved to feed her rabbits carrots and lettuce and watch them nibble the food and wiggle their noses. Heather took such good care of the rabbits that they multiplied. Soon she had a lot of baby rabbits. She had so many that she gave the babies away to other kids, so they could have pet rabbits too.

Natasha took the leaping lizard home. She found an old whipped cream container, put the leaping lizard in it, and put the lid on. But Natasha didn't take very good care of the lizard. She put the whipped cream container into a drawer and then forgot about it.

One day Mr. Cobble came back to town. He wanted to see how his pets were doing. He visited Carlos's house first.

"Oh, Mr. Cobble," Carlos said, "it's so good to see you again!"

"It's good to see you too, Carlos," Mr. Cobble agreed. "How are those fish doing?"

"They're doing great!"

Mr. Cobble looked at the aquarium and saw

that it was full of fish. He smiled. "You did just fine," he said, patting Carlos on the back.

Next Mr. Cobble went to Heather's house.

"Hi, Mr. Cobble!" Heather said.

"Hello, Heather. How are those rabbits doing?"

"Great!" she said. "They even had babies, which I gave away to other kids so they could have pet rabbits too."

Mr. Cobble looked in the cage and saw the furry rabbits hopping around. "You've done a wonderful job taking care of them," he said, patting Heather on the head.

Finally, Mr. Cobble went to Natasha's house.

"Hi, Mr. Cobble!" Natasha said. "What are you doing here?"

"I came to see how the leaping lizard is doing."

"The leaping lizard? Oh no!" Natasha ran from the room. When she came back, she was holding a whipped cream container in her hand. She opened it up.

The leaping lizard wasn't leaping anymore. He was very sick.

"Natasha," Mr. Cobble said, "what happened to the lizard?"

Natasha shook her head. "I guess I forgot to take care of him. I just put him in this container and then put it away in a drawer."

Mr. Cobble frowned. "Well, Natasha, a leaping lizard can't leap very well when it's closed up in a container like that."

"I guess you're right," Natasha said.

Mr. Cobble nodded. "I think I'm going to have to take the lizard from you because you can't take care of it. Carlos and Heather took very good care of their pets, and the pets multiplied. But you didn't take very good care of your pet, and he got very sick."

Natasha's eyes filled with tears. "I'm sorry, Mr. Cobble."

Mr. Cobble smiled. "I think the lizard will be OK. I'll take him to the veterinarian right away." Mr. Cobble was quiet for a minute, then said, "You know, Natasha, just like I gave you and Carlos and Heather these pets, Jesus gives us all gifts, or things we are good at. Jesus wants us to use our talents so they can multiply and bless others. We shouldn't hide away our talents, like you did with the lizard. We should take care of them like Carlos and Heather took care of their pets. Can you think of anything you're good at?"

Natasha thought for a moment. "Well, I'm learning how to play the piano right now."

"That's wonderful! If you take good care of that talent by practicing every day, maybe someday you'll be able to play the piano in your church. Then all the people at church will enjoy your beautiful music."

"Yeah!" Natasha said. "That would be great! But I guess if I ever want to play in church, I should take better care of that gift than I did of the lizard." She looked down at the lizard in the whipped cream container. He stuck out his tongue, and Natasha laughed.

"I think the lizard agrees with me!"

———————————————

Don't fail to use the gift the Holy Spirit gave you.
1 Timothy 4:14

The Little Church Builder

A Story about Following Jesus

Heather lived at the top of a hill in a big house surrounded by green shade trees, with a large pool in the backyard. Heather had her own room, a beautiful canopy bed, lots of dolls, and toys, toys, toys.

One day, at a tea party at Heather's house, Heather's friends admired all these beautiful things. "You have such a big room," one girl said.

"I wish I didn't have to share my room with anyone," another girl added.

"Well," Heather replied, "I owe it all to God." She really wanted to give credit where it was due.

The girls had a great time playing with all of Heather's nice things. But soon it was time for them to go home. After they had left, Heather's mom came into her room and said, "Let's talk."

Mom looks pretty serious, Heather thought. She had a feeling something special was about to happen but had no idea what it could be. "What do you want to talk to me about?" she asked anxiously.

"You love Jesus, don't you, Heather?" Mom asked.

"Yes."

"And you love him with all your heart?"

"Yes, Mom, of course I do. Why do you ask?"

With a hug, Mom said, "I know you do, because you're one of the best little girls a mother could ever hope to have. You clean your room, you listen, and you try to help whenever you can. You're such a good daughter."

"Thanks, Mom," Heather said. "Is that all you wanted to tell me?"

"No, that's not all." Mom smiled and took a deep breath. "Well," she said, "your father and I have been given a chance to help others by working across the country. We're going to move to Washington and help start a church!"

"Washington?" Heather said, shocked. "I've never been to Washington!"

"I know," Mom answered. "It's a big move, and we'll have lots of changes. For one thing, we're going to live in a smaller house."

"A smaller house!" Heather gasped. "Will I have my own room and a pool? Will I be able to take all my toys?"

"You can take some toys, but I'm afraid we're going to have to get along without all the nice things that we have now," Mom said.

"For how long?" Heather asked, almost not wanting to know.

"For at least the first few years," Mom replied. "But maybe longer."

"A few years! That's so long! Do we have to go?"

"Yes, Heather, we need to go. Your dad and I feel it's what God wants us to do."

Heather was very angry. Without saying another word, she walked outside. She found her dad gardening on his hands and knees in a flower bed.

"Dad," she cried, "I don't think it's a good idea to go to Washington."

Dad looked up at Heather. "Why do you say that?" he asked tenderly, hugging her.

"Well, I have so many friends here, and I don't want to leave them. Plus, I don't want to give up my nice things."

"I understand," Dad said as he wiped the dirt from his hands. "I know it will be difficult to move. But I really believe this is what Jesus wants us to do."

"Well, can't Jesus find someone else to go?" she asked sharply.

"What if we're that someone else?" he asked. "I feel in my heart that Jesus wants us to go."

He brushed off his clothes, then walked over to the patio table and sat down. Heather sat down beside him. On the table was a book about Washington. Dad opened up the book and showed Heather the pictures of its mountains and people.

"Aren't there enough churches in the world without starting another one?" Heather asked impatiently.

"There are never too many people spreading the good news about Jesus," Dad answered.

"Well, I don't want to go," Heather said angrily. She stood up and ran to her room. She closed the door and stayed there, refusing to come out for supper. She decided that she was not going to eat that night, or any other night, as long as they were going to Washington.

Later that evening, Dad walked into her room and sat on her bed. "I want to tell you a story," he said. "Once when Jesus was preaching with his disciples, a young man came up to him and said, 'Master! Master! What do I have to do to have eternal life?'

"Jesus knew the young man loved him. 'Well, my friend, you must obey your parents,' Jesus said.

"'Master, I've done this all my life,' the young man replied.

"'Then' Jesus said, 'you shouldn't steal or lie.'

"'I've never stolen anything, Master,' the young man insisted. 'I don't lie. I try my best to do all the things God requires me to do.'

"Jesus saw that this young man meant what he was saying. Jesus loved him very much. So he said, 'Sell all you have and follow me.'

"The young man was very rich. He owned a brand-new chariot with strong horses, and he had expensive clothes. He said, 'Sell all I have? You mean give up my chariot, my horses, my servants, and my expensive clothes?' He noticed that Jesus was very poor, then sadly said, 'I don't think I can do that.'

"The young man walked away very sad. He had everything except Jesus."

Dad looked at Heather. "Do you understand what I'm trying to say?" he asked. "The Lord has blessed you with so much, but if it stands in the way of following Jesus, then it's not good."

Heather thought for a moment, then said, "You mean if God wants us to go to Washington, then I shouldn't worry about my clothes, my room, and my dolls?"

"That's right, Heather," Dad replied. "If we put him first, all these other things won't matter as much."

Heather smiled, then turned to Dad and said softly, "If you and Mom believe that going to Washington is what Jesus wants us to do, then I want to go too. I'll be his church builder. I want Jesus to be first, and I don't want to make him sad or ever lose him. I'll even give up my toys and dolls if I have to."

Heather's father threw his arms around her and gave her a kiss. "You," he told her, "are the real doll!"

[Jesus] expects you to follow in his steps.
1 Peter 2:21

The Lemonade Sale

A Story about Giving

Natasha had a savings account at the bank. For a long time, she had been saving her allowance and birthday money from her grandparents to buy something special for herself. She didn't know what she wanted to buy, but she was sure that when she saw it, she would know.

One day, Natasha saw a bicycle in the bike shop. It was the most beautiful bike she had ever seen. "That's it!" she said to herself. "That's what I want to buy with my money."

So Natasha ran home and found her mom.

"Mom! Mom! Remember the money I've been saving? Well, I just saw a bike that I want to spend that money on."

Natasha's mom was busy vacuuming the floor. She turned off the vacuum and looked at Natasha. "Well, dear," she said, "if you're sure that's what you really want, you can use your money to buy the bike. How much does it cost?"

Natasha's face went blank. "Oh no! I forgot to ask," she said.

So she ran back to the bike shop. By the time she got there, she was all tired out.

"Mr. Herbert?" she asked, taking a deep breath. "Mr. Herbert, how much is that bike?" Natasha pointed toward the window. In it sat a new bicycle with all the latest features. It sparkled as the sunshine reflected off the glowing red paint.

Mr. Herbert, the store owner, smiled. "Yep, that's a real beauty," he said. "I'll tell you what. You can have that bicycle for . . . sixty dollars. It used to be eighty-five."

"Wow! Thanks, Mr. Herbert!" Natasha said. And just as quickly as she had run in, she ran out.

When she got back home, she found her mom dusting. "Mom! Guess what? The bike only costs sixty dollars. It used to be eighty-five!"

Mom set down her dust rag. "That certainly is a good deal, Natasha. But I'm afraid you only have fifty-five dollars in your savings account."

"Well, can you give me five more dollars, then?" Natasha asked.

Mom shook her head. "Remember, Natasha, that I said you could get whatever you wanted, but that you had to raise all the money yourself."

"But, Mom, I only need five more dollars!"

"I'm sorry," Mom said, "but that was our agreement. Dad and I want you to learn about saving and responsibility. I suggest that you wait to buy the bike until you have five more dollars."

"But where can I get five dollars? It'll take me forever to save it. The bike might be gone by then."

Mom smiled. "Well, why don't you see if you can earn it," she said as she began dusting again.

Earn it? Natasha thought. *How on earth can I earn five dollars?*

Then suddenly she had an idea. "Mom!" she yelled. "Do we have any lemonade in the house?"

"We sure do," Mom answered.

So Natasha ran into the kitchen and grabbed the lemonade mix. She quickly mixed it with water and sugar in a big glass pitcher. Next, she took a chair and dragged a table out in front of the house. Then she made a sign with a piece of paper and an orange marker that said "Lemonade 50¢." Natasha was in business!

"Boy," she said as she fanned herself with her hand, "this is a good day to sell lemonade. It's hot out here!"

Pretty soon, some kids from the neighborhood rode by on their bikes and bought lemonade. And grown-ups in cars stopped to buy lemonade too. After a couple of hours, Natasha had earned five dollars and fifty-five cents. That was enough to buy the bike!

After she put away the lemonade, the table, and the chair, she and her mom went to the bank and got her fifty-five dollars. Then Natasha ran with the money to the bicycle shop.

When she got there, a woman was talking to Mr. Herbert.

Come on, hurry up, lady, Natasha thought to herself. *I've got to get this bike. I don't want to wait forever. Hurry up, please!*

The woman continued to talk to Mr. Herbert. "The local churches are collecting money for the starving children in Africa," she was saying. "Thousands of children are dying, and we need to collect as much money as possible. Would you be able to help out today?" She smiled.

Mr. Herbert smiled back. "Of course!" he said. "I'm always willing to give to a good cause." He wrote out a check for the woman and gave it to her.

As the woman put the money away, she

turned around and noticed Natasha. "Would you like to help the children in Africa too?" she asked.

Natasha hesitated. "Uh, I would, but I don't have any money right now," she said. *I can't give her my money,* she thought. *That's for my bike!*

"Well, all right, dear," the woman said. "Thank you for waiting so patiently to talk to Mr. Herbert."

After the woman left the store, Mr. Herbert turned to Natasha. "OK, what can I do for you?" he asked.

"I've got the money for the bike," Natasha said proudly as she pointed to the money in her pocket.

"My, you certainly want that bike, don't you?"

"Yeah, I sure do."

Mr. Herbert went to the window and removed the brand-new, shiny red bicycle. "Here it is," he said as he placed it before her.

"And here's your money," Natasha said as she counted out the money. "Five, ten, twenty, twenty-five, thirty-five, fifty-five . . ."

Suddenly, she stopped counting. She was quiet for a long time.

"Mr. Herbert, I'll be right back," she finally said as she picked up the money off the counter.

Natasha ran down the street. "Wait! Wait!" she yelled. Finally, she caught up to the woman who was helping the children from Africa.

The woman turned around and saw Natasha. "Yes, what is it?" she asked.

"I'm sorry," Natasha said softly. "When I said I didn't have any money, I lied. I do have money. I wanted to use it for something else, but I think the starving children in Africa are more important than my bike. Here's five dollars and fifty-five cents."

"My, that's a lot of money. Where did you get this?" the woman asked.

"I sold lemonade to earn money for my bike," Natasha said shyly.

"Well, God bless you. This is a very nice thing to do."

Natasha slowly walked back to the shop and

went inside. "Mr. Herbert you can put the bike back in the window," she said. "I don't have enough money anymore."

"I don't understand, Natasha."

"I gave five dollars to the lady who was raising money for the children. I'm sorry that I wasted your time."

Natasha turned around to leave, but before she could walk through the door, Mr. Herbert called her back. "Natasha, wait. The bicycle is now fifty-five dollars."

"Huh?" Natasha said in surprise. "You said it was sixty dollars."

"I know," he said, smiling. "I just dropped the price to fifty-five."

"Wow!" Natasha couldn't believe her ears. "But why did you drop the price?"

"Well," Mr. Herbert said, "I'm very impressed that you gave away some of your money like that. And I think God is happy too. He wants us to give to people that don't have as much as we do." He smiled. "But I wanted to make sure that you still got your bike."

Mr. Herbert took the bike and gave it to Natasha. She sat on the seat and put her hands on the handlebars. Then she reached into her pocket, took out the money, and started to count again. "Five, ten, twenty, twenty-five, thirty-five, fifty-five. Here you go Mr. Herbert—fifty-five dollars."

After Mr. Herbert gave her a receipt, Natasha walked the bike out of the shop. Then she jumped on and began pedaling home. She was so happy. Not just because she had a new bike, but also because she knew that the money she had given would help other kids across the world.

It is more blessed to give than to receive.
Acts 20:35

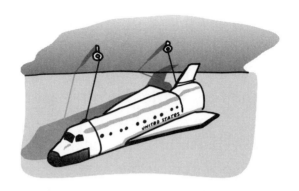

The Divided Room

A Story about Brotherly Love

Phillip thought his little brother, Carlos, was a pest. Carlos was always following him around. Every place he went, there was Carlos, walking right behind him, walking right beside him, or walking right in front of him. Carlos also used Phillip's stuff without asking. "If only I didn't have to share a room with that pest," Phillip often would say to himself.

One day, Phillip walked into his room and saw Carlos lying on his bed. He was reading a sports magazine and had his feet propped up on Phillip's pillow.

"Hey!" Phillip shouted. "Get off my bed!"

Carlos rolled his eyes. "What's the big deal? Who cares if I'm on your bed? It's softer than mine, anyway."

"Get off! I don't want to see you on my bed, or with my stuff, or touching anything that belongs to me," Phillip said in an angry voice. "Do you understand?"

Carlos threw down the magazine and jumped off the bed. "You're mean!" he yelled as he stomped out of the room.

Phillip was glad Carlos had left the room. He didn't like sharing his room with such a pest. He never got to be alone; Carlos was always there. And Carlos was always touching his stuff.

Then Phillip had an idea. He took some big, thick, black tape and rolled the tape right across the center of the room, making a line between his side and Carlos's side. *This ought to keep him away from my stuff,* Phillip thought.

When Carlos came back, Phillip pointed to the line of black tape. "You see this line?" he said to Carlos, who was standing in the doorway. "This is my side of the room, and that side is yours. I don't want to see you on my side of the room—ever! Do you understand? If you touch anything of mine, or if I see you on my side—Boom!" Phillip clapped his hands together.

Carlos didn't say anything. He just made a gulping noise.

"Do you understand, Carlos?" Phillip said in his scariest voice.

"Yeah, I understand."

"Good. I'm going downstairs to get a snack, but when I come back, I better not find you on my side."

But a little while later, when he came back into the room, Phillip couldn't believe his eyes. There was Carlos, standing on top of the bookshelf! He had one foot on Phillip's history book and the other on a crumpled poster of the Chicago Bears football team. Carlos was reaching for the model space shuttle that hung from the ceiling. Phillip had put that shuttle together a year ago. He was very proud of the good job he had done putting it together. He did NOT want Carlos to touch it!

"Hey! Carlos!" he yelled.

"Uh-oh," Carlos said as he turned his head and saw Phillip frowning at him.

"What are you doing up there? I thought I told you to stay on your side of the room."

"But I just wanted to look at your space shuttle model," Carlos said.

"I told you not to touch my stuff! I'm going to get you!"

But before Phillip could say another word, Carlos jumped from the bookshelf to the dresser, then sprang to the bed. Then he dashed across the room and out the door. Phillip ran after him and chased him all the way downstairs.

"Mom, Mom! Help!" Carlos yelled as he ran into the kitchen.

"What's the matter?" Mom asked as Carlos quickly dropped to the floor and slid between her legs, like a baseball player sliding into home plate.

"I'm going to get you," Phillip said as he followed Carlos into the kitchen.

"Mommy, he's going to beat me up," Carlos cried from behind Mom's skirt. "He's going to get me!"

"What's going on?" Mom said. She didn't look happy.

"Carlos is always touching my things and bugging me," Phillip explained.

Mom reached down and scooped Carlos to his feet. "Are you being a pest?" she asked him.

"Of course not, Mommy," he said sweetly.

"Well, I don't know about that. Listen, I want you boys to try to get along. I'm sick of all your arguing and fighting." She pointed her finger at the two of them, then walked out of the room.

Phillip waited until Mom was gone, then whispered, "Next time, I'm going to get you, Carlos." He took his left hand, made it into a fist, and slammed it into his right hand. The slapping sound of his two hands meeting together echoed across the kitchen. Carlos looked scared. *Good, I'm glad he's scared,* Phillip thought as he walked away.

He wandered into the garage, looking for his baseball glove. Then he noticed his dad's brand-new fishing pole hanging on the wall. His dad loved to fish, and so did he. He took the pole off the wall and went into the backyard. The touch of the rod brought back memories of the times when just he and Dad would go fishing for hours and hours.

Phillip cast out the line, then reeled it back in. Or at least he tried to reel it back in. Then he noticed that the hook was caught on the drain pipe of the garage roof. He pulled and pulled, but the hook wouldn't come loose. He yanked on the pole one more time, and it snapped!

Oh no! I broke Dad's new fishing pole! What am I going to do? he thought. He knew he wasn't supposed to play with Dad's stuff without asking for permission. He didn't want to get in trouble, so he quickly picked up the pieces and hid them in the garage where no one would find them.

But what Phillip didn't know was that someone had seen him break the fishing pole. Carlos had been looking out his bedroom window and had seen the whole thing!

Later that day, at supper, Phillip didn't have an appetite. He didn't eat any of his chicken. He just stared at his mashed potatoes. He didn't even laugh when his baby sister, Ann, took a handful of peas and threw them on the floor. He felt so guilty for what he had done.

But Carlos seemed very happy. He ate all of his food. "Can I be excused? I'll be right back," he asked after he had cleaned his plate.

"Sure," Dad answered.

When Carlos returned, he had the broken fishing pole in his hand. "Look what I found," he said with a smile.

Dad looked very angry when he saw his brand-new fishing pole broken in two.

"Phillip did it," Carlos said as the bobber fell and landed in Phillip's mashed potatoes.

Phillip wanted to disappear from the room. He tried his best to blend in with the chair he was sitting on. Then he slowly began to sink beneath the table, wishing he was anywhere else but where he was.

"Did you do this, Phillip?" Dad asked. He sounded angry.

"Yes, he did," Carlos quickly answered. "Didn't you, Phillip?"

Phillip was now underneath the table, with Baby Ann's spilled peas.

"Phillip," Dad said, "I want you to get up from underneath that table right now."

Phillip slowly stood up. Dad looked at him and Carlos.

"Both of you come with me," Dad demanded as he also stood and made his way out of the dining room. When they were all in the next room, Dad turned to look at them. "I'm very disappointed in you two," he said in a deep voice.

"Me? Why me?" Carlos asked. "Phillip was the one who broke the fishing pole!"

"I'm disappointed in Phillip for touching something that doesn't belong to him," Dad said. "But I'm also disappointed in you because you wanted Phillip to get in trouble. Mom told me that you guys have been fighting a lot lately. Why is that?"

Carlos and Phillip looked at each other. Phillip knew Dad was right. They *had* been fighting a lot lately.

"I saw that line in your room," Dad continued. "And it doesn't take a genius to figure out why it's there. I want it removed. Is that understood? And you are both grounded for a week."

"A week!" Carlos squeaked.

"Would you like me to make that two weeks?" Dad asked.

Phillip shook his head. "No, Dad, one week is good."

"All right, then," Dad said. "I want the two of you to go up to your room and think about how brothers should treat each other. God wants us to love other people, and that includes your brother."

So Phillip and Carlos went up to their room and took off the black tape. Phillip knew Dad was right. He and Carlos were brothers. They should love each other.

He walked over to a chair and pulled it over to where his space shuttle model hung from the ceiling. He stood on the chair and reached for the model.

"Hey, what are you doing?" Carlos asked.

"You said you wanted to see my space shuttle, right?" Phillip replied. "I'm taking it down so you can look at it."

"You are? Why?"

"Because you're my brother, and I love you. But could you do me a favor?" Phillip asked.

"Sure. What?"

Phillip grinned. "Could you show me some brotherly love next time and ask first?"

Love each other deeply, from the heart.
1 Peter 1:22

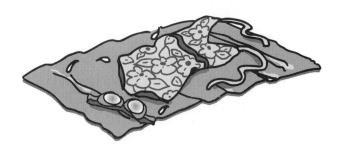

A Friend in Need

A Story about Persistence

The doorbell rang just as Melissa was eating breakfast.

"Come in!" she yelled from the kitchen table.

Natasha walked into the house. "Come on, Melissa, we've got to get going," she said.

"Just two more gulps," Melissa said before finishing her orange juice. Then she put her breakfast dishes into the dishwasher and grabbed her gym bag. She followed Natasha out the door and into the car Natasha's mom had pulled into the driveway.

"Are you girls ready for swim practice?" Natasha's mom asked.

The girls nodded their heads and smiled. They loved to swim. Both of them were on a swimming team, and their moms took turns driving them to practice.

Today Melissa and Natasha were especially excited to go to swim practice. They were practicing for a swim meet competition. Only a few of the fastest swimmers from their team would compete. Today they would learn who would be chosen.

When Melissa and Natasha got to the pool, they raced to where the results were posted.

"Oh, Natasha, Natasha!" Melissa said, jumping up and down. "Look, there's my name! I made it into the competition! I made it!"

But as she turned to Natasha, Melissa saw only a sad face. Natasha looked and looked but didn't see her name on the list. She wasn't fast enough. She wouldn't get to swim in the competition.

"Oh, Natasha," Melissa said. "I'm so sorry."

"Me too," Natasha said. Tears filled her eyes.

Melissa was sad for Natasha, but Natasha didn't seem happy for Melissa. She began to ignore Melissa. Pretty soon, she hardly talked to her at all.

Now Melissa felt even more sad. At practice a few days later, Melissa faced Natasha. "You hardly talk to me or play with me," she said. "Aren't we still friends?"

"Why would you even want to be friends with a turtle?" Natasha asked, looking away.

"A turtle? What do you mean?"

"You swim so much faster than me—you make me feel like a turtle," Natasha explained. "So why do you want a pokey turtle for a friend?"

"You're not a turtle," Melissa said. "You're a good swimmer too. I was just lucky this time. Can't you be happy for me?"

Natasha shook her head. "Maybe if you swam slower, like me," she said.

Melissa didn't know what to say. She watched her friend walk over to another group of swimmers. She wanted Natasha's friendship, but she wanted to do her best at the competition too. She decided to just keep trying at both.

On the day of the competition, Melissa went over her plan as she rode her bike to school. Right after school, she would pedal over to the swimming pool. It wasn't too far away, and she would give herself plenty of time. Then she could relax and prepare for the race.

Things seemed to go as planned when, after school, Melissa ran to her locker to pack up her stuff. Only then did she notice that something was missing!

"My swimsuit!" she screamed. "I forgot my swimsuit. I left it at home!" Her words echoed in the hallway.

Melissa ran to her bike and pedaled home as fast as she could. *How could I have forgotten my swimsuit?* she thought. *Without it, I can't compete.* But she had been so excited that morning, with lots of things going through her mind. *Will I have to give an acceptance speech if I win? Will there be another competition after this one? If I win, will Natasha ever be my friend again?*

Halfway home, Melissa remembered that her mom was going to meet her at the pool after running errands. *Oh no!* she thought. *The house will be locked. But I can't be late!* She looked at her watch. It was three fifteen. She had just forty-five minutes before the swim meet started!

Melissa was just about to give up when she thought, *I need a friend.* Then she said to herself, "Natasha! Natasha lives close by, and she's my size. Maybe she'll let me wear her swimsuit!"

She jumped on her bike and pedaled as fast as she could to Natasha's house. When she got there, she looked at her watch. It was three twenty-five. *I don't have much time,* she thought. She ran to the door and knocked.

"Natasha!" she yelled. "Natasha, Natasha!" She rang the bell and tapped on the window.

Finally, Natasha came to the door. "Oh, hi, Melissa," she said. "What do you want?"

"A terrible thing happened," Melissa said, still

out of breath from the bike ride. "I've got to get to the competition today by four o'clock, but I forgot my swimsuit! I left it at home."

"So go home and get it," Natasha said, looking away.

"I can't do that. I can't get in the house or reach my mom. I need to borrow your swimsuit, Natasha. Can I, please? Can I?"

Natasha frowned. "Why would you want the swimsuit of a turtle?" Then she shut the door in Melissa's face.

Melissa was so sad. *What am I going to do?* she thought. *Maybe I'll have to swim in my clothes.* She started to walk away. Then she remembered something her dad had told her. "God doesn't want us to give up," he had said. "We need to be persistent. That means that when we need something, we should keep on praying to him."

So Melissa said a prayer. "Please, God," she prayed. "Please help me be a friend to Natasha just like I want her to be a friend to me. Oh, and God? I wanted to do my best today. If that's what you want too, help me find a way." Then she went back to the house and knocked on the door again. "Natasha, I'm so sorry if I've hurt you in any way. I've always wanted to do my best—and to be your friend. Please let me use your swimsuit."

"Not in a million years," Natasha said through the door. "Go away. You don't want the swimsuit of a turtle."

By now it was three thirty. Melissa only had a half hour before the competition began. But she didn't give up—she knocked on the door again. "Natasha! Please, open the door. PLEASE! I'm not going to give up until you open this door. I'm going to stay here and bang and bang and bang, even if I miss the competition!" Melissa yelled at the top of her lungs.

Finally, Natasha opened the door.

Melissa sighed. "You're my good friend, Natasha, and I need your help. You're right—I don't want to borrow the swimsuit of a turtle. I want to borrow the swimsuit of a friend, and I want you to be my friend more than anything."

Natasha had her swimsuit in hand. "Go ahead and take it," she said, smiling. "I was missing you as my friend too, but it hurt not getting to swim in the competition. I guess I was only thinking about myself."

"Oh, thank you!" Melissa said. She looked at her watch. "But what am I going to do about the competition? I'll never get to the pool in time on my bike."

Natasha's eyes lit up. She grabbed Melissa's hand and ran to her mom's car, which was just pulling up in the driveway. "Mom, Mom!" she called out. "The swim competition is today at four o'clock, and if Melissa isn't there, she won't be able to race. She needs to get there right away. Can you give her a ride?"

"Sure!" Natasha's mom said. "I can do a little racing too." She winked at the girls as they fastened their seatbelts, then took a shortcut they'd never known of before—without speeding.

They arrived at the pool with fifteen minutes to spare! Melissa jumped out of the car, with Natasha right behind her.

"I'm sorry for the way I acted, Melissa," Natasha said. "It wasn't a very nice way to act. I really hope you do well today—and that you'll forgive me."

"Always!" Melissa said with a smile. "Because if you didn't ask me to be your friend again, I'd keep bugging you into it."

"Well," Natasha said, grinning, "I guess that's what friends are for."

"That," Melissa said, "and spare swimsuits!"

Ask, and it will be given to you. Search, and you will find. Knock, and the door will be opened to you.
Luke 11:9

A Shining Light

A Story about Being a Witness

Heather was lonely. She and her parents had just moved across the country, to a state called Washington. They had moved there to start a new church. Starting a new church was hard work, but Heather's parents were happy doing it, because they knew they were doing what God wanted them to do. But Heather was not happy.

She tried to be brave in her new surroundings because she wanted to please her parents. And she wanted to do the will of Jesus. But this didn't keep Heather from being lonely. She felt that she just didn't fit in with the other kids in the neighborhood.

One day, Heather sat on the front steps of her new house in Washington, feeling sorry for herself. "This just isn't fair," she said to her mom. "I wish I were back home. I don't like this small house. I wish I were back with my old friends."

Mom looked at Heather. "Well, we've been living here for quite some time, but you don't seem to be very friendly with the other kids in the neighborhood. You need to make some new friends."

"But I don't want new friends, Mom!" Heather whined. "I miss Natasha and Danny and Michael and Carlos. Besides, the kids here talk and act different from the kids back home. I just don't think I like it here."

"Heather, I know it's hard moving to a new place and making new friends. But you've got to try. And remember, a lot of the kids in this neighborhood don't know Jesus yet. Remember the song 'This Little Light of Mine'? You need to let your light shine so other kids can learn about Jesus. You need to be a witness to them."

"I know," Heather sighed. She looked down the

street and saw a girl about her age sitting on a front porch, just like she was. *Maybe I can go make friends with her,* Heather thought. She got up and walked down the street. When she stood in front of the girl's house, she lifted up her hand and waved.

"Hi," she mumbled.

The little girl didn't say anything. She didn't look at Heather either. Heather waved again.

But again, no response. "Well," Heather said to herself, "here I am, trying to make a friend, and this little girl just ignores me. That's the last time I try to make friends with these kids!" She stomped back to her house. She was very angry. She would've liked to take the next plane out of there!

"What's the matter, Heather?" Mom said when Heather plopped back down on the front steps. "I thought you were going to make friends with that little girl."

"Yeah, but she didn't want to make friends with me," Heather said.

"Well, what did you say to her?"

"I just waved and said 'hi.'"

"Oh dear," Mom said. "I think I know what the problem is. That must be the blind girl who lives in the neighborhood. She must not have seen you wave. Why don't you go over and talk to her this time?"

Heather didn't want to go over and talk to her. What would they talk about? After all, she had never known a blind person before. She was a little bit afraid.

"Well, go on, Heather," Mom said. "Go on over and talk to her."

So Heather stood up and slowly walked over to the blind girl's house. She walked closer and closer until she was right next to the girl. Heather stood there, looking at her for a long time. Then, to Heather's surprise, the little girl spoke up.

"Aren't there any blind girls where you come from?" she asked.

"Huh?" Heather said.

"You must be the new girl on the street," the blind girl said with a smile.

"Huh? How did you know I was here?" Heather said with a gasp.

"Well, I heard you walk up. Even though I'm blind, I can still hear, you know. What's your name?"

"Heather." Heather was quiet for a moment, then said, "Does it hurt?"

"Does what hurt?"

"Being blind," Heather answered, feeling a bit foolish.

The girl thought for a moment. "It only hurts my feelings sometimes, when other kids stay away from me and treat me differently."

Heather felt bad, because that's exactly what she had done. But she decided that she did want to know the girl better. "What's your name?" she asked.

"Sheela."

"Nice to meet you, Sheela."

Sheela was quiet for a moment, then said shyly, "Do you want to be my friend?"

Heather had never been friends with a blind person before. But she liked Sheela, so she said, "Sure! I'd love to be your friend."

Heather and Sheela spent the rest of the afternoon laughing and talking. They talked about their families, school, dolls, and lots of other things. Heather had so much fun!

Then she saw her mom down the street, waving to her. "Uh, I think I have to go home, Sheela," she said. "My mom's waving at me. It must be time for dinner."

Sheela smiled. "OK. I'll probably have to eat soon too. Do you want to come over again tomorrow?"

"Sure!" Heather said. She stood up and started walking away. Then she remembered something her mom had said earlier that day. She turned around.

"Hey, Sheela," she said. "My parents are helping to start a church in the neighborhood. Do you want to come to church with me on Sunday?"

"Yeah!" Sheela said happily. "I've never been to church before. Thanks for inviting me!"

"You're very welcome," Heather replied. "That's what friends are for!"

Lead a life of love, just as Christ did. . . .
Live like children of the light.
Ephesians 5:2, 8

The Big Surprise

A Story about Heavenly Rewards

Mr. Roberts was outside working in his yard when he heard the telephone ring. He ran inside to answer it.

"Hello?" he said.

"Hi, Dad. It's me, Jack."

"Hi, son," Mr. Roberts said. "Getting ready to leave for the airport?"

"Uh, sorry Dad," Jack replied. "The weather here is really bad. None of the planes are able to take off today. We won't be able to leave for your house until tomorrow."

"Oh," Mr. Roberts said. His son, Jack, was calling from a long ways away. Jack was going to take his family to visit Mr. Roberts, but now, because of the bad weather, they wouldn't be able to leave until tomorrow. Mr. Roberts was disappointed. He had been planning on taking his grandkids to the circus that night.

"I'm really sorry, Dad," Jack said. "We hope to get there tomorrow. The kids are very excited to see you."

"I'm excited to see them too," Mr. Roberts said. "I bought tickets for the circus tonight because I thought the kids would like to go."

"Oh no!" Jack said. "I'm sorry, Dad. What are you going to do with the tickets?"

"Well, maybe I can get a refund for them," Mr. Roberts replied. "I'll solve that problem later, though. Hope to see you tomorrow. Bye, son."

Mr. Roberts hung up the phone, then thought, *It's too late to get a refund for those tickets. I better find someone to give them to. But first, I should get to the supermarket to buy some snacks for tomorrow when the grandkids get here.*

Mr. Roberts headed outside and began walking to the supermarket. While he was walking, he saw Danny and Michael sitting by the curb. They didn't look very happy.

"Hey, guys!" he said to the two boys. "Why are you looking so sad?"

"Oh, we're just bored. Bored, bored, bored," Danny replied.

"Yeah, we've got nothing to do," Michael added.

"Hmm," Mr. Roberts said. He stopped for a moment to think, then an idea came to his mind. "Well, I'll tell you what. How would you like to do a job for me?" he asked as he sat on the curb next to the boys.

"A job?" they repeated at the same time.

"That's right. And at the end of the day," Mr. Roberts added, "I'll give you a big surprise."

"Oh, wow, Mr. Roberts! What is it? What is it?" they asked with excitement.

"If I told you, then it wouldn't be a surprise, now

would it?" Mr. Roberts said with a smile. Then he added, "I have some odd jobs around my house that need to be done today, and it looks to me like you guys are just the men for the job. C'mon, I'll show you what to do."

Two hours later, while Danny and Michael were working, Mr. Roberts went out to visit his neighbor. As he was walking down the street, he saw Carlos throwing a ball against his garage door.

"Hi, Mr. Roberts," Carlos said.

"Hello," Mr. Roberts replied with a smile on his face. "Isn't this a beautiful day?"

"Yeah," Carlos agreed. "But I sure wish I had somebody to play with. My brother went away for the week, and I'm bored without him here."

"I'm sorry to hear that," Mr. Roberts said. "Hey, I've got something to keep you busy. I have two fellows doing some work at my house, and you may join them if you like. Then, at the end of the day, I'll give you a big surprise."

"Really? Cool!" Carlos said. "What's the surprise?"

"I can't tell you. It wouldn't be a surprise then, would it? C'mon, I'll show you what to do."

Later that afternoon, while Danny, Michael, and Carlos were working, Mr. Roberts got another telephone call. It was his neighbor, who wanted to know if Mr. Roberts could take care of his little boy, Timmy, for a few hours.

"Sure!" Mr. Roberts said. "Send him right over. I've got some other boys doing yard work for me, and Timmy can join them."

So when little Timmy came over, Mr. Roberts put him right to work with Danny, Michael, and Carlos. Since the day was almost over, there wasn't much left for Timmy to do, but he did his best.

An hour later, at the end of the day, Danny, Michael, Carlos, and Timmy all went to get Mr. Roberts. "Come on, Mr. Roberts!" they said. "Come see the good job we did."

Mr. Roberts went out and inspected his garage. It was clean as a whistle. He went out and looked at his yard. The grass was nicely cut and trimmed.

He went out to the patio area, and all the equipment was put away neatly.

"My goodness," Mr. Roberts said. "You boys did a fine job! A really fine job." He noticed the boys smiling with self-satisfaction. He knew they were eager to receive their surprise, so he went inside to get it.

When Mr. Roberts came back, he had all the boys line up in front of him. Then he took out some tickets from a large white envelope.

"Here you go," Mr. Roberts said to the boys. "You all get tickets to the circus tonight."

"Wow! Thanks!" the boys said. But suddenly Danny and Michael did not look happy.

"Wait a minute! Hold everything," Michael said to Mr. Roberts. "You gave Carlos the same thing you gave me and Danny. He came two hours later, so he didn't work as long as we did."

Now it was Carlos's turn to look unhappy. "Well," he said to Mr. Roberts, "you gave Timmy the same thing you gave me, and he came at the end of the day. He didn't work nearly as long as any of us. Why does he get to go to the circus?"

Mr. Roberts folded his arms across his chest. "You're right. None of you worked the same amount of time as the others. But whose tickets are they?"

"Well, they're yours," Danny said reluctantly.

"That's right. They're my tickets, and I can do with them as I please. I promised you all a big surprise for the job you did, and I kept my end of the deal."

"Well, this doesn't seem right, because we didn't put in the same amount of work," Danny complained.

"That's right, you sure didn't," Mr. Roberts agreed. "But why are you upset with me for being kind to each of you?"

The boys looked at each other. They didn't know what to say.

"Let me tell you something," Mr. Roberts said. "I've been a Christian my whole life. But I have a friend who just became a Christian a year ago.

When I get to heaven, do you think I should be mad that my friend is there too? After all, I was a Christian much longer than he was."

"Well, no," said Carlos. "You should be happy that your friend is in heaven."

"That's right," said Mr. Roberts. "Just like no matter how long you worked, you got a ticket to the circus, God gives heavenly rewards to people, no matter how long they were a Christian."

The boys all smiled. "I guess that's a good thing," Michael said. "And I guess we should be happy that we all get to go to the circus."

Michael was right. They all went to the circus that night with Mr. Roberts—and they all had a great time!

Everyone who calls on the name
of the Lord will be saved.
Romans 10:13

Lunch Money

A Story about Loving Your Enemies

Michael didn't want to go to school. Not because he didn't like school. He liked school just fine. He liked his teacher, he liked math class, and he especially liked playing with his friends at recess. What he did not like was Kevin, the meanest boy in class, taking what wasn't his.

Kevin was a bully. He was mean to everyone. Sometimes he even called people names. But the worst thing was that every day Kevin stole somebody's lunch money.

Today, Michael hid his lunch money in his

shoe. "Kevin will never find it there," he said to himself.

But when he got to school, there was Kevin, waiting for him.

"Hey, Mikey," Kevin said with a frown. "Give me your money."

Michael tried to act brave, but Kevin was big and scary. "Sorry, Kevin," Michael said, trying to keep his voice from shaking. He patted his pocket. "I guess I didn't put my money in my pocket today." Michael tried not to feel guilty. He wasn't exactly lying. He hadn't put his lunch money in his pocket—he'd put it in his shoe.

"Oh yeah, right," Kevin said. "I don't believe you." He reached over and felt Michael's pockets. "All right, the money's not in your pockets. But what about your shoes?"

Michael gulped. "My shoes?"

"Yeah," Kevin said. "Take 'em off."

Michael slowly took off his shoes. Sure enough, there was his lunch money. Kevin bent over and picked up the money.

"Thanks, Mikey," he said with a smile. "You better not tell any teachers about this."

Michael clenched his fists as he watched Kevin walk away. He was so mad! Why did Kevin have to be so mean? He decided he would be more careful tomorrow. Not only was he taking lunch money to school the next day, but he also was taking some of his own money. He and his friend Natasha were going to buy some baseball cards after school.

Michael tried to think of a better place to hide his money. "I know!" he said to himself. "I'll put it in my sock. Kevin will never find it there."

At school the next day, Michael looked for his friend Natasha on the playground.

"Hi, Natasha!" he whispered. "I brought some extra money to school today so we can buy baseball cards. I just hope Kevin doesn't take it."

"Yeah," Natasha agreed. "He's so mean."

Just then, Michael's older brother, John, walked up to them. "Did I just hear you say that Kevin has been taking your money?" John asked.

"Yeah," Michael said. "But we're not supposed to tell anyone, or Kevin will beat us up. He's so mean!"

"Well, why don't you try being nice to Kevin?"

"Be nice to him!" Michael said in surprise. "Why should I be nice to him, when he's so mean to me?"

John smiled. "Don't you remember what Dad always tells us? God wants us to love our enemies and to treat them the way we want them to treat us."

All morning during class, Michael thought about what John had said. Maybe he should try being nice to Kevin. Maybe Kevin would be nice back.

When the bell rang for recess, Michael took off his shoe, reached into his sock, and pulled out his lunch money. Then he looked at his baseball card money, which was still stuffed down in his sock. He pulled that out too.

He walked over to Kevin. "Hi," he said. "Do you want to eat lunch with me today? I have some extra money, so I could buy you something too."

Kevin looked at him in surprise. "Why do you want to eat lunch with me?"

"Well, because I thought maybe we could be friends," Michael said.

Kevin shrugged his shoulders. "OK, Mikey."

So Michael and Kevin headed to the cafeteria. Michael bought chicken nuggets, apples, and milk— enough for two lunches. Then he sat down next to Kevin.

"I love chicken nuggets," Michael said.

"Me too," Kevin agreed.

"Oh, you love all food," Michael said in a teasing voice.

"Yeah," Kevin said, laughing.

Michael tried to think of something else to say. After a moment of silence, he said, "My dad works at a bank. What does your dad do?"

Kevin was quiet for a minute, then said, "My dad lost his job a while ago. He's not working right now." Kevin looked like he was about to cry.

"Is that why you take people's lunch money?" Michael asked. "Because you don't have your own?"

Kevin nodded. "I just don't want other kids to

know. I guess that's why I act so mean sometimes. I don't want them to think I'm a loser."

"You're not a loser unless you act like one," Michael said. "It's not bad to need money or help, but it is bad to be mean."

Kevin shrugged. "Yeah. I guess you're right."

Michael reached for another chicken nugget. He started to eat it, then waved it in front of Kevin. "Now, this chicken here is the real loser," he said.

Kevin laughed. "Yeah, I guess he could've used a friend like you!"

Love your enemies. Pray for those who hurt you.
Matthew 5:44

About the Author

Hey, guys! My father asked me to write this since he is too shy to do it himself . . .

Joel Thompson is the author of the ClubZone Kids book series. At his youthful age (he asked me to put that in), he is also the creator of the *CMJ ClubZone* TV show from SonBurst Media and helped create the *BloodHounds, Inc.* TV series. He's starred in many New York Broadway shows, written and produced national TV commercials (my favorite was for Arby's), appeared on *The Tonight Show* and some show called *The*

Merv Griffin Show, written songs for grown-ups like Perry Como and Nell Carter, was a television producer and began at the famous award-winning Public Television hub WGBH Studios in Boston, and was a member of the New Christy Minstrels (whoever they are).

He graduated with honors from Charles E. Mackey Elementary School in Boston, where he was voted class clown four years running and elected President of the Hall Monitors of America Association. He was an excellent newspaper boy and still found time to sell his used comic books to neighborhood kids.

Best of all, my dad—oops! ahem—Joel is also an ordained minister who speaks to churches and at conferences. He's not at all ready to settle down to one job. He wants to do and create too many things before he really grows up!

His all-time favorite food is "anything with cheese," and the real loves of his life are God, his wife, Vicki, and family, our cocker spaniel, Coco, and, of course, ME!

Heather Marie Thompson

About CMJ ClubZone

More than 2.4 million fans tune in weekly to *CMJ (Come Meet Jesus) ClubZone* from SonBurst Media, a 30-minute national children's television program that reinforces faith, positive values, and self-esteem through a relationship with Jesus.

The show features Artie's Treehouse, the Curious Cam Man (portrayed by Joel Thompson), who investigates kids' questions with his video camera, and the ClubZone Kids, a diverse cast of talented youths who

- learn amazing facts about nature and archaeology
- sing lovable, positive songs
- discuss faith and values, and

- meet special guests like neurosurgeon and best-selling author Ben Carson *(Gifted Hands)*, star athletes from the Detroit Lions and the Green Bay Packers, plus doctors, judges, artists, educators and ministers from across America who share valuable insights from diverse professions in kid-friendly language.

Each of the season's 26 shows focus on a specific theme discussed by real kids. Music, laughter, drama, suspense, and Scripture follow, drawing young viewers closer to Jesus.

More than 10 additional independent networks around the globe carry the show, including The Inspirational Network, TCT, World Harvest Television, Total Living, Cornerstone TV, Dominion Sky Angel, Angel 1, Kids and Teens TV, MBC, and Australian Christian—reaching more than 42 million TV homes per week, and in some cases daily.

For more information about the TV series, videos, the *Kids Are Christians Too!* radio program and other extensions of the CMJ ClubZone interfaith, nonprofit ministry, write to . . .

CMJ ClubZone
P.O. Box 400
Niles, MI 49120

www.cmjclubzone.com

Follow the CLUBZONE KIDS

Through All Their Adventures...